This book is dedicated to all of His children...

STERLING CHILDREN'S BOOKS
New York

An Imprint of Sterling Publishing Co., Inc.
1166 Avenue of the Americas
New York, NY 10036

Text © 2010 Tom Roberts
Illustrations © 2009 Doug Moss

ISBN 978-1-4549-3673-2

Distributed in Canada by Sterling Publishing Co., Inc.
c/o Canadian Manda Group, 664 Annette Street
Toronto, Ontario M6S 2C8, Canada
Distributed in the United Kingdom by GMC Distribution Services
Castle Place, 166 High Street, Lewes, East Sussex BN7 1XU, England
Distributed in Australia by NewSouth Books, University of New South Wales
Sydney, NSW 2052, Australia

For information about custom editions, special sales, and premium and corporate purchases,
please contact Sterling Special Sales at 800-805-5489 or specialsales@sterlingpublishing.com.

Manufactured in China
Lot #:
2 4 6 8 10 9 7 5 3 1
07/19

sterlingpublishing.com

SANTA'S PRAYER

A Story by Tom Roberts
Illustrated by Doug Moss

STERLING CHILDREN'S BOOKS
New York

It was on Christmas Eve

In a small Midwestern town
During the late afternoon
And the snow was coming down

When my sister and I

Had gone for a walk

Down the ol' church road

To have a Christmas talk

We wondered aloud
About *reindeer and elves*
About candy-filled stockings
And presents for ourselves

We talked about getting
Our wish list of toys
About dear old Santa
The focus of our joys

When there at the church
We saw a flash of red
Of a figure going inside
With white hair on his head

We knew in an instant
It was the ol' man himself

Mr. Kris Kringle

That great jolly old elf

So, we snuck in behind him
To see what he would do
And we *watched* and we *listened*
While crouched behind the pew

He stood there for a moment
And so quiet all the while
Then he took off his hat
And started down the aisle

He walked up to the altar
And knelt there in the hay
Right beside the manger scene
Where the infant Jesus lay

He bowed his whiskered face
He closed his twinkling eyes
Then he began to speak
And much to our surprise

He prayed to baby Jesus
In a voice so soft, yet clear
So, sister and I moved closer
To make sure that we could hear

He said, "Dear Jesus - thank you
Thank you *for this night*
Thank you *for who you are*

And for your Christmas light

I come to you this Christmas
With a **concern** on my mind
A concern for the children
And what they expect to find

When tomorrow morning comes
And the gifts are handed out
Will they still remember
What Christmas is all about?

I pray that you will guide me
As I make my rounds this eve
To bring some understanding
With **every present**
that I leave

Understanding to the children
That the toys from *Santa's sleigh*
Are only fleeting fancies
Rarely lasting beyond the day

I pray that you will bless me
With the **knowledge** that I need
To help all of these children
To not give in to greed

To recognize that Christmas
Is not all about me
Or pretty wrapped packages
Placed beneath a tree

I pray that they'll remember
That you're the inspiration
The **true reason**
for the season
The Christmas celebration

You're the **star** of Christmas time
And should be throughout the year
You're the one who deserves the praise
Not ol' Santa here

I am just your servant

Helping however I can
To remind all the children
Of the gift you gave as man

Your life and your love
And the example you have shown
Are gifts that'll last forever
Long after they are grown

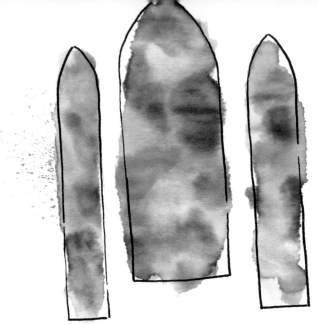

So, help me dear Lord
    Help me make it clear
        To all the world's children
                That you're the focus here

I pray that they'll **be thankful**
And feel your love within
Then share the joy of Christmas
And let hope spring forth again"

It was then Santa paused
And grew silent for a time
When suddenly from above
We heard the church bells chime

Taking a deep breath
   Santa raised his burly head
   And ending his humble prayer
   This is what he said, . . .

"Well, dear Jesus, it is time
Ol' Santa must now depart
But, I'll be thinking of you *always*
I'll keep you in my heart"

Then opening his eyes
Santa rose to his feet
And with a glow on his face
He walked to the street

Sister and I stood silently
Watching him leave in awe
Then we turned to the manger scene
Where Jesus lay in the straw

We looked at one another
We didn't know what to say
But, when we saw the little babe
We felt like we should pray

So, we knelt down beside Him
Unsure of what to do
Then we remembered Santa
And said,

"Dear Jesus – thank you!"